The Chocolatier's Apprentice

An Echo Memoirs Book

This book was created in celebration of Purdy's 100-year anniversary.

This book is dedicated to all of the people who have poured their hearts into creating delicious chocolates at Purdy's for the last 100 years.

Purdy's would like to thank the following sponsors for making this book possible:

Ivanhoe Cambridge and their participating properties:

Guildford Town Centre	Oshawa Centre
Mayfair Shopping Centre	Southcentre
Metropolis at Metrotown	Southgate Centre
Oakridge Centre	Sunridge Mall
Oakville Place	Woodgrove Centre

***

TELUS

***

CanWest Global Communications Corp.

***

Echo Memoirs

***

All profits from the sale of this book will go to Raise-a-Reader, an award-winning national program designed to increase awareness and raise money and resources in support of family literacy programs.

***

ISBN 0-9781811-3-1

Book design by Erin Anderson

Printed in China

Commissioned by Purdy's Chocolates
2777 Kingsway, Vancouver, BC V5R 5H7
www.purdys.com

Published by Echo Memoirs
#302 - 70 East 2nd Avenue, Vancouver, BC V5T 1B1
www.echomemoirs.com

The Chocolatier's Apprentice

Written by Victoria Miles
Illustrated by Lee Edward Födi

If there was ever anyone who might make his mark in chocolate...

...it was Eli Edward Earnest Puddicombe.

For as long as he could remember, Eli Edward Earnest had dreamed of being a chief of chocolate... a captain of cocoa...a chocolatier.

5

Eli always got a double-decker chocolate cake with fudgey frosting for his birthday. The rest of the year there was pie or pudding for dessert. Which was fine, but it was not chocolate.

But every year for Christmas, Uncle Elgin Puddicombe gave Eli's mother a beautiful box of chocolates. And it was Puddicombe tradition that Eli was allowed to choose the first one.

In those days, Eli was not much of a sampler. His fingers went straight for a round chocolate with a swirl on top – the signature of his best beloved in the whole box...
the chocolate-covered chocolate cream.

His next step was to nibble off the dark shell in pursuit of his favourite part: the milk chocolate centre. This he ate with his own peculiar combination of unhurried happiness.

After the last trace of the cream centre had melted from his mouth, Eli would always look hopefully at his mother. "Chocolate is a treat, Eli," she would say gently. "Go play."

Now, perhaps not surprisingly, Eli's favourite thing to play was chocolate. On hot summer days, he made make-believe mud chocolates, marshmallow marbles-in-mud, even molded mud medallions – all very sploodgey to look at and terrible to taste. Which he did. A few times. Just in case there was a chocolate fairy somewhere with a bit of magic in her wand meant for Eli.

Eli learned to read by reciting the legend tucked inside the chocolate box. The Christmas he was five years old, he astonished his Puddicombe parents by sounding out the entire list: ca-ra-mel...cor-di-al...marsh-ma-llow...mar-zi-pan...

Which, if you were to ask them, was about the time Mr. and Mrs. Puddicombe noticed that their Eli Edward Earnest was very, very serious about chocolate.

In high school, Eli wrote chocolate cookbook reports, and history reports about the ancient Aztecs and their chocolate drinks. He won the school science fair for his project "Why chocolate is good for you." The prize? A scholarship to any school in the world.

Any school? Any one at all? Perhaps this boy had a chocolate fairy after all.

At chocolate school Eli, a most serious student, learned an alphabet of work in chocolate.

"A" was for Adding the cream to the mix. "B" was for Blending the chocolate until smooth. "T" was the toughest. "T" was Tempering. Tempering meant heating, cooling and then reheating chocolate so that it would be excellent for eating: firm, shiny and snappy. Eli poured warm chocolate from a bucket over a marble table, then scraped and turned the chocolate until it thickened and cooled to just the right temperature. If he let it get too cold, the rest of the chocolate in the bucket would seize up lumpily when he added it in. He could've used a thermometer, but master chocolatiers relied on the touch of a finger to tell them if the heat was right. Eli had to re-melt and try again hundreds of times before his fingertips were foolproof.

DEAR E

LOVE MOM

16

Eli's first job after chocolate school was in the country's finest chocolate factory.

19

Great shipments of chocolate arrived from America and Belgium at the factory doors every day. Driving a forklift, Eli stacked crates filled with chocolate slabs that would be melted and mixed into the factory's secret recipe. And he stacked boxes of finished chocolates ready for the shops. Cartons of creams and caramels, coconut snowballs, mocha melties, almond clusters, raspberry jellies, peppermint wafers, milk chocolate macadamias, peanut-butter daisies, foil-covered fudgies and dozens and dozens of other specialties.

The stacks could only be so high, there could be no tipping.

20

Eli, being Eli, took all this stacking very seriously.
And all this lugging and tugging made him very strong.

Very, very strong.

21

One afternoon, as Eli was leaving for the day, Mac White, the head chocolatier, called out to him: "Get a good sleep tonight! I've got a special job for you!"

Eli was elated. Would he finally be invited into the candy kitchen? Could it be the beginning of cooking cream fillings? Fixing fudge? Mixing meltie bars?

Ah, but in fact, four hundred sacks of peanuts had arrived. Four thousand pounds to be unloaded and stored... all in one day.

If Eli was disappointed, he never said. He just set to, and the mountain he'd made by the end of the day was a marvel to see. Fortunately, no one marveled more than Mac. The very next day, he rewarded Eli with the job of loading great slabs of chocolate into the main melting vats. Hundreds of the heavy

slabs went in one at a time, until 10,000 pounds of dark and milk chocolate were blended together, then passed through the ceiling pipes to machines throughout the factory. **And the smell!** It was like standing in a chocolate sauna, breathing in warm, chocolate air.

As word of Eli's strength spread, he was called to the kitchen every day by the other chocolatiers to lift and pour kettles of caramel, batches of creams and buckets of chocolate into beaters. Soon he was starting every morning in the candy kitchen, and at last, a few weeks before Easter, Mac finally handed him the apron of an apprentice.

27

Within days the factory was bursting with bunnies. At his peak, Eli was molding 5,000 a day. There were molds small enough to make hand-sized rabbits and molds for bunnies almost as tall as Eli. With serious concentration, he gave them all pretty much the same dizzying beginning, pouring warm chocolate into molds, sealing them tight and then giving them a slow spin. No bubbles allowed. Nobody wanted a bunny full of bubbles. Once they'd cooled down in their molds, the chocolate shrunk just a tiny bit and out popped the rabbits, ready for wrapping.

HAPPY EASTER
PHILBERT!
~FROM ELI

And what happened after Easter? Eli was sent to the stringing line. Stringing, he thought, was like being a puppeteer. If he made his fingers dance in the right direction he could swirl curling letters atop the chocolates, or, by touching their tops very lightly he could make little patterns, two-at-a-time, as rows of chocolates trundled down the conveyor belt. With cheerfully choreographed twiddles and twirls the crew taught him how to make the factory's symbols to top the chocolate-covered creams.

But he wasn't on the stringing line for long before Mac came up with his next assignment.

"Taming the tiger!" he told Eli, handing him a little rake. The job was tiger butter. Eli remembered tiger butter from chocolate school. Tiger butter was tricky.

Mac helped Eli pour and spread peanut butter cream over a long table. Eli was nervous. There was no re-melting and trying again with tiger butter. If the stripes were messy he'd have botched the whole thing. Quickly and carefully he squirted chocolate all the way down the stretch of cream. The hardest part came next. Drawing his rake crosswise through the chocolate over and over again, he made the pattern that gave tiger butter its name. And when it was cool, he cut it into sharp, perfect squares.

Mac grunted. He made some notes. He grunted again. Mac had never met anyone who tamed the tiger on the first go. Mac studied his clipboard.

This Eli was something special. True, he was something serious, but he was special.

"Pack your bags, Eli!" said Mac. Eli looked seriously confused. Were the stripes uneven? Had he messed up? Where was an apprentice's chocolate fairy when he needed her?

"Pack your bags!" said Mac again, gleefully.
"Tomorrow, we fly to France!"

Oh, thought Eli, there she is.

Everywhere they went, factory doors were proudly opened to Mac and his team of curious chocolatiers. First, in France, Eli sampled petite squares of dark, dark chocolate. Scarcely sweet and perfect for a pixie, they suited Eli's style of studious appreciation.

In Belgium, Eli saw for the first time the beginnings of the great slabs of chocolate he had spent so many hours dropping in the melting vats back home. In Switzerland, Eli was hypnotized by the conching machines that plowed deep, velvety pools of molten chocolate into perfect smoothness.

In Germany, Eli practiced painting marzipan – making pale peaches blush, giving rosy cheeks to green apples, brightening yellow bananas...

DIE-LICIOUS

DER LEHRLING

Dear Philbert:
I hope you like these treats from Italy!
ELI

P. HEDGEHOG

In Italy, Eli spread thick chocolate-hazelnut paste on his toast for breakfast. And in one tiny town, he bought a bag of cone-shaped, cream-filled chocolates the people called "Pinocchio's noses."

And in England, Eli's teeth got stuck together on a chocolate toffee bar.

All in all, it was the best time he'd ever had.

No sooner was Eli back at the factory than he began to experiment. He mixed chocolate with spicy peppers, green cardamom, curry and cayenne, cinnamon and chilies. Mac, a maple-walnut man at heart, looked a little doubtful. Was this just a chocolatier's natural curiosity, or was Eli one step away from attempting chocolate-covered cabbage?

But secretly Eli was frustrated. Seriously. While many of his spicy experiments were...well, interesting, he didn't delight in them. Not the way he felt when he was a boy, nibbling his Christmas chocolate cream. That was what he wished for and yet it seemed that for the first time in his life, the harder he tried, the more bothered he became.

And then one day, after botching a batch of brittle, Eli remembered what his mother used to say:

"Chocolate is a treat," he whispered to himself.

43

"Go play."

So that night, after everyone else had gone home, Eli played.

Not seriously.

Just for the fun of it.

46

And I tell you, what he made that night is still talked about in the factory to this day. And yes, absolutely, it tasted as good as it looked. Everyone said so.

Which is as it should be with chocolate. And just what would make a true chocolatier very happy.

And Eli Edward Earnest Puddicombe was a true chocolatier.